Final Exodus-Part Two
The Reckoning

About the Author: Nacovin J. Norman, Sr.

Nacovin Norman is an educator, activist, and author dedicated to empowering marginalized communities through education, advocacy, and storytelling. Drawing from history, sociology, and political science, he challenges systemic barriers and promotes justice through his work.

His fiction, including *Final Exodus: Rising Truth* and *From the Streets to Galilee*, intertwines historical struggles with contemporary issues. His nonfiction works, such as *The Lost Leadership* and *Cultural Identity and Mental Health*, address systemic challenges in education and leadership. His academic research explores media's impact on racial attitudes and multiculturalism.

A passionate advocate for labor rights and educational justice, Norman emphasizes collective action and community empowerment. His work serves as both a blueprint and a call to action, inspiring individuals to critically engage with systemic issues and drive meaningful change.

Final Exodus-Part Two
The Reckoning

By Nacovin J. Norman, Sr., ED.S.

Copyright © 2025 by Nacovin J. Norman, Ed.S.

All rights reserved.

No part of this book may be reproduced, distributed, or transmitted in any form or by any means, including photocopying, recording, or other electronic or mechanical methods, without the prior written permission of the author, except in the case of brief quotations embodied in critical reviews and certain other noncommercial uses permitted by copyright law. For permission requests, write to the author at the contact information below:

Self-Published by: Nacovin J. Norman, Ed.S.

Cherry Hill, New Jersey

Email: Nacovin@gmail.com

This is a work of fiction. Names, characters, places, and incidents are either products of the author's imagination or are used fictitiously. Any resemblance to actual events, locales, or persons, living or dead, is entirely coincidental.

Printed in the United States of America

First Edition, 2025

To my dearest nephew and godson,
Jace A. Macnair,
May you always chase your dreams with unwavering determination, knowing that the journey is as important as the destination. Embrace challenges as opportunities to grow, and remember that your family stands beside you, cheering you on every step of the way.

With all my love and faith in you,

Your Uncle and Godfather

Nacovin Sr.

Final Exodus

Through shattered dawn and veiled disguise,
A people rise with burning eyes.
The earth still hums with echoes deep,
Of names once lost, but never asleep.

The rivers whisper of stolen past,
Of kingdoms high and shadows cast.
Through chains of time, through bitter sands,
They march unbowed with open hands.

A prophecy in blood is drawn,
The veil is torn, the night is gone.
No silence now, no breath restrained,
No hidden truth shall be contained.

Through fire, through storm, through fractured stone,
They carve a road to claim their own.
No tyrant's hand, no master's lie,
Can drown the voice that fills the sky.

The reckoning is here at last,
No longer ghosts of buried past.
They stand as thunder shakes the land,
A final exodus at hand.

Introduction: The Reckoning Has Come

There has always been a struggle over who controls the narrative. The power to define history, to name heroes and villains, to dictate what is remembered and what is erased—this has always been the battle behind the battles. But today, that battle is no longer confined to dusty archives or quiet rooms of power. It is unfolding in real-time, waged across institutions, communities, and digital landscapes. The forces that have long dictated the terms of identity and belonging now find themselves in a desperate scramble to contain what has already begun: an awakening too powerful to suppress, a reckoning too urgent to ignore.

The tides of truth are rising, yet those who have long profited from silence are working harder than ever to muddy the waters. They brand awareness as extremism, paint justice as division, and disguise suppression as order. To be *woke*—to be conscious, aware, and unwilling to accept the world as it is—has been twisted into an insult, turned into a weapon wielded against those who refuse to remain asleep. They want compliance, not questioning. They want obedience, not remembrance. They want us to forget, to believe that our story is one of endless struggle with no redemption, no reclamation, no return. But memory is a force more powerful than oppression. And the memory of a people cannot be erased so easily.

For centuries, entire peoples have been uprooted, their histories rewritten, their very identities fractured into pieces too scattered to reassemble. We have been told that our past is lost, that our lineage is a mystery, that we are products of chance rather than continuity. We have been taught to accept a world where our ancestors' sacrifices are footnotes and our contributions are mere afterthoughts. But history is not the property of the oppressor. It belongs to those who lived it, those who carried it forward despite every effort to erase them. It belongs to those who remember.

Yet, history is not just about what has been done to us—it is also about what we *choose* to do with it. Recognition alone is not enough. Reflection alone is not enough. To awaken to the truth and do nothing is a betrayal of those who fought to preserve it. The question before us is not whether we will remember, but whether we will *act*. Will we let the truth collect dust, confined to academic debates and whispered conversations? Or will we wield it like the weapon of liberation it was always meant to be?

This book is not just a story—it is a reckoning.

It is about those who refuse to be content with symbols of progress while the structures of oppression remain intact. It is about those who reject the illusion of representation as a substitute for real power. It is about the fight for identity in a world that thrives on burying it.

In *Final Exodus: The Reckoning*, the battle for truth stretches across continents, from the streets of America to the heart of Jerusalem. It is a war between those who seek to reclaim what was stolen and those who will stop at nothing to keep them dispossessed. It is a struggle against those who would rather burn history than allow it to be reclaimed. It is about those who see justice as a threat, who label resistance as radicalism, who weaponize fear to maintain their grasp on power. But their time is running out.

This is about more than a movement. It is about more than identity. It is about existence itself. Those who have been oppressed have always understood that their very presence is an act of defiance. Their breath, their joy, their ability to love, to create, to build, to persist—this, too, is resistance. But the time has come for more than endurance. The time has come for reclamation. For restoration. For exodus.

What happens when the forgotten begin to remember? When the silenced refuse to stay quiet? What happens when those who were scattered find their way home, not just in body, but in spirit, in truth, in purpose?

To those who believe the fight for justice is over—this book is a warning.

To those who believe history is settled—this book is a disruption.

To those who seek truth beyond the narratives they were given—this book is an invitation.

To those who fear what is coming—this book is your reckoning.

The *Final Exodus* has begun.

Will you awaken?

THE RECKONING BEGINS

Final Exodus – Part Two   Nacovin J. Norman, Sr.

Table of Contents

Chapter One: The Unveiling 2

Chapter Two: The Gathering Storm 10

Chapter Three: The Hidden Ones 15

Chapter Four: The First Assembly 22

Chapter Five: The Awakening and the Cost 40

Chapter Six: Into the Unknown 52

Chapter Seven: The War Goes Public 59

Chapter Eight: The Fall of Empires 66

Chapter Nine: The Gathering of Nations 72

Chapter Ten: The World At War 79

Chapter Eleven: The War for Truth 86

Chapter Twelve: The Trumpet Sounds 93

Appendix: The Biblical, Historical, and Scientific Case for the Descendants of Slavery as Israelites...100

Chapter One: The Unveiling

Jerusalem, Camden, and Miami – The Night of the Blackout

Part One: The Truth That Could Not Be Hidden

Jerusalem – The International Biblical Conference

The air inside the Israel Institute of Biblical Archaeology was dense, carrying the scent of old paper, polished wood, and an unshakable undercurrent of tension. The grand lecture hall, its arched ceiling amplifying every hushed murmur, was filled beyond capacity. Academics, theologians, journalists, and skeptics sat shoulder to shoulder, their eyes flickering between curiosity and quiet resistance. Some had come to affirm what they already knew. Others had come with the singular intent to dismantle what was about to be revealed.

Amina Bediako gripped the podium, steadying herself. She had stood in front of audiences before—published, debated, dismissed—but tonight was different. This wasn't just a lecture. This was the culmination of decades of research, a confrontation with history itself.

She exhaled slowly and clicked to the next slide.

"What you see before you is the culmination of over twenty years of study, tracing genetic migration patterns, Y-DNA markers, mitochondrial haplogroups, and linguistic connections between the ancient Israelites and the African diaspora."

The projector hummed as the massive screen behind her illuminated, displaying an intricate genetic map. Colored lines stretched across continents, overlaying modern West Africa with ancient trade and migration routes. Pulsating highlights pinpointed regions—Ghana, Nigeria, Senegal, the Ivory Coast—each marking a historical fingerprint, a fragment of a lineage that had been intentionally severed from collective memory.

A murmur rippled through the crowd.

"We have long been told," she continued, her voice unwavering, "that the transatlantic slave trade erased our past. That our history began in chains. That our ancestors were nameless, displaced people—stateless and identity-less."

She let the words settle before clicking again. The next slide revealed direct genetic correlations between the Lemba people of Southern Africa, the Beta Israel of Ethiopia, and Black Americans whose DNA bore markers originating from the Levant.

"We were not lost," Amina declared, her voice ringing clear over the restless murmuring. "We were scattered."

From the edge of the room, **Rabbi Yitzhak Levi** watched, arms folded tightly over his chest. His face remained unreadable, but his eyes burned with an emotion Amina recognized—vindication, long overdue.

Then—the lights went out.

The hum of the projector died. The air-conditioning stilled. Darkness swallowed the hall in an instant. Gasps echoed. Chairs scraped against the floor as silhouettes shifted uneasily.

Then, the doors slammed open.

Amina froze.

Someone screamed.

Figures emerged from the shadows, moving with military precision, their silhouettes barely visible against the dim emergency exit lights. They were not ordinary disruptors. These men belonged to something older, something structured, something ruthless.

The Obscured had arrived.

Camden, New Jersey – The Pastor Who Knew Too Much

The old walls of Zion Missionary Baptist Church groaned against the winter wind, the stained-glass windows casting dim colors against the office walls. Pastor Sam Matthews sat in his chair, back straight, fingers hovering above his laptop's keyboard. The glow from the screen illuminated his face, deepening the creases in his brow. His breath was steady, but beneath his calm exterior, his heart pounded against his ribs.

He had lived through decades of struggle—he had fought against redlining, voter suppression, the quiet dismantling of Black economic power. But tonight, what he had just seen on that screen shook him to his core.

Amina's voice had carried across the livestream, clear even through the grainy feed. The proof was there. The truth was undeniable. A history hidden in the fabric of scripture, buried under centuries of systemic erasure, was unraveling before his eyes.

Then—the screen cut to black.

His pulse spiked. He checked his phone. No signal. The router's blinking red light confirmed what he already feared.

Offline.

The stillness in the room thickened, wrapping itself around him like a noose. His fingers curled into fists, the weight of realization pressing down on him. They had been watching. Waiting.

Then—three slow, deliberate knocks on the church's side door.

Sam exhaled. He reached for the wooden bat that leaned against the desk, his fingers curling around the worn handle. He had dealt with threats before—

hate mail, vandalism, intimidation tactics from local authorities. But this felt different. The air shifted, thick with an unseen force, the kind that made the hairs on the back of his neck stand on end.

"Who is it?"

Silence.

The knock came again, the weight of it heavier, more insistent.

His mind raced. He thought of Marcus, his son. If something happened to him tonight, Marcus would be alone. But he had always told his boy, *we do not live in fear. We stand in truth.*

His grip tightened around the bat as he rose to his feet, moving cautiously toward the door. The bat felt solid in his grasp, but it did nothing to steady the churning in his gut.

Then—the doorknob turned.

Miami, Florida – The Trap is Sprung

The heat in the community center was suffocating, made worse by the packed room and the thick tension pressing down on the crowd. The energy had shifted the moment the broadcast cut out.

Miguel Rivera stood near the back of the room, every muscle in his body coiled, his instincts screaming at him. He had grown up learning how to read a room. It was survival.

And this room felt wrong.

The whispered prayers and hushed conversations had given way to anxious murmurs, faces lit only by phone screens, searching for an answer that wasn't there. No signal. No connection. Just dead air.

"They did it," Miguel muttered under his breath.

Beside him, Rosa's brows furrowed. "Who did what?"

Miguel's jaw tightened. He turned to her, his voice low. "They just killed the feed. They're coming."

Rosa inhaled sharply, her hands clenching into fists. The air felt charged, like the thick stillness before a thunderstorm.

Then—the double doors at the front of the center burst open with a force that rattled the walls.

Men in black, their faces obscured by tactical masks, moved in with cold precision. Not police. Not local gangs.

Something worse.

The room erupted into chaos. People scrambled, chairs overturned, screams cut through the heavy air. Miguel's instincts took over. He grabbed Rosa's wrist and pulled her toward the back exit, weaving through the panicked bodies. The crowd was a shield, a momentary distraction.

A gunshot cracked through the air.

Miguel turned sharply. One of the masked men had stepped forward, his gun still raised, his voice eerily calm despite the pandemonium around him.

"Miguel Rivera."

Miguel didn't blink.

The man smirked beneath his mask. "Come quietly."

Miguel flexed his fingers. He had two choices—surrender or fight.

Not a chance.

Prophecy Unfolding

Three cities. Three warriors.

In Jerusalem, Amina ran for her life.

In Camden, Sam prepared to fight.

In Miami, Miguel stood his ground.

And somewhere in the unseen realm, the heavens stirred.

"For there is nothing covered that shall not be revealed, neither hidden that shall not be known."
(Luke 12:2, LXX)

The war for the truth had begun.

Chapter Two: The Gathering Storm

Transition: The Spread of the Conflict

What had begun in Jerusalem was not an isolated event. Across the world, the shadows of The Obscured were moving, tightening their grip on those who dared to unveil the past. As the lights flickered out in that ancient hall, another battle for truth erupted in the heart of Camden. And in Miami, far from the old world's sacred stones, another life was about to be upended.

The war had begun, and none of them would face it alone.

Part One: Shadows of Jerusalem

The Old City lay beneath the weight of night, cloaked in a silence that was both ancient and alive. Shadows stretched long across the uneven stone paths, the moon's pale glow turning the timeworn alleyways into a labyrinth of silver and shadow. The air carried the faint scent of incense, distant spices, and the cold breath of history, mingling with the remnants of whispered prayers still lingering at the Western Wall.

Amina Bediako moved like a ghost through the passageways, her breath tight, controlled. The weight of her satchel dug into her shoulder, the leather strap creaking softly with every hurried step. Behind her, the city lay deceptively still. Yet she knew she was not alone.

She had felt them before she had seen them—their presence like a shift in the air, unseen eyes pressing against her back. The men who pursued her were not common enforcers; they moved with the precision of hunters trained in the art of silence. The Obscured. She had underestimated their reach, the depth of their presence. They had infiltrated institutions, dictated historical narratives, erased truths—and now, they had set their sights on her.

Her mind churned, not just with fear, but with betrayal. For years, she had believed that the pursuit of knowledge—truth—would be enough. That academia, for all its flaws, still harbored those who sought enlightenment, not suppression. Yet, as she ran through the same streets that had carried the feet of prophets and scholars, she realized the depth of her naivety. The system had never been built to find the truth—it had been built to bury it. And she had just unearthed something they could not allow to see the light of day.

She stopped near an arched doorway, pressing her back against the cold limestone. Her heartbeat pounded against her ribs, steady but insistent. Carefully, she peered into the darkness she had just left behind. The alley lay empty, its silence a trap. A lone lantern flickered at the corner, casting erratic shadows that shifted with the wind. Then—a movement. A shape detached itself from the deeper dark, fluid and controlled.

Amina swallowed her fear. If she hesitated, she would not get another chance.

She pushed off the wall and ran.

Her feet struck the ancient stone in rhythmic urgency, weaving through the narrow alleys with a familiarity born from years of study. The city's architecture twisted upon itself—passageways leading to abrupt dead ends, stairways climbing into rooftop pathways only to descend into courtyards hidden from the modern world. It was a city built by time, a sanctuary for those who knew its secrets.

Her pursuers knew them too.

The footsteps behind her did not falter, their pace neither hurried nor reckless. They moved with the certainty of men who had already decided the outcome. She had studied them in theory, dissected their tactics through historical accounts of missing scholars and unexplained disappearances. Now, she was part of that history.

Amina turned sharply into a covered passageway, the scent of old wood and stone filling her lungs. Ahead, the alley curved toward the Armenian Quarter, its streets deserted at this hour. She needed to disappear, to find cover before they closed in. The weight of her satchel pressed against her side. The documents within—historical records, genetic data, undeniable truths—were already out in the world, copies sent to those who would understand their significance. Yet The Obscured did not want the papers. They wanted the woman who had dared to unravel their work.

A sudden noise snapped her focus. A door creaked open just ahead, a woman stepping out into the night with a basket of laundry, her movements unhurried, oblivious to the chase playing out around her. Amina veered left, slipping beneath an awning, narrowly avoiding an overturned cart. A shout rang out from behind her, the first sound her pursuers had made all night. They were closing in.

Her mind raced through escape routes. She needed higher ground.

The passage ahead opened into a small courtyard, its paving stones worn smooth by centuries of footfalls. Across it, a stairway spiraled upwards into darkness. Amina did not hesitate. She took the steps two at a time, lungs burning, muscles coiling with effort. At the top, the path spilled onto a flat rooftop overlooking the slumbering city, its domes and minarets bathed in moonlight. The Dome of the Rock gleamed in the distance, a silent witness to history's cycles of conquest and revelation.

She paused for only a moment, breathing hard. Then—the sound of pursuit. Heavy footsteps striking stone. She turned. Shadows moved below, then surged upward, closing the gap between them.

Amina stepped to the edge, her mind calculating distances, angles. The rooftops formed a jagged web of possible escape routes, each one carrying its own risk. A wrong move meant a broken limb, a captured prize. She glanced back once, saw the first of them crest the stairway, their figures dark against the sky.

The Obscured had no uniforms, no insignias. Their distinction lay in their precision, their silence, the way they moved with an uncanny coordination, as if bound by something deeper than training—ideology. She had read about factions within their ranks, those who disagreed on how much to suppress, how much to reveal. Had she reached one of those limits? Were there those among them who questioned why she was being hunted? If there were, she would never know.

There was no more time.

With a whispered prayer, she leapt.

The wind caught her as she landed on the adjacent rooftop, knees bending to absorb the shock. She rolled, came up running. Behind her, the hunters reached the edge and hesitated—but only for a moment. One of them followed.

The chase was no longer silent.

Breathless, heart pounding, Amina ran, weaving through the night's uncertain paths. The storm behind her was growing, and the city of Jerusalem, with all its ancient wisdom, held its breath to see if history would be rewritten once more.

Chapter Three: The Hidden Ones

Jerusalem, Camden, and Miami – Converging Paths

Part One: The Underground of the Holy City

Jerusalem – Amina Bediako

The air was damp, thick with centuries of forgotten prayers and whispers of the past. Amina Bediako moved carefully, her footsteps muffled against the stone floor of the ancient tunnel. The walls, chiseled by hands that had long since returned to dust, curved inward slightly, pressing against the space around her, swallowing sound, swallowing light. Her breath came slow and steady, but her pulse still thrummed beneath her skin, a constant reminder that she was not safe. Not yet.

She didn't know exactly how far she had run. She had lost count of the turns, the streets, the rooftops she had leapt across before slipping into the underbelly of the city. The Old City of Jerusalem was a labyrinth above ground, but beneath it, it was something else entirely. A place of refuge for some, a tomb for others. Her hands grazed the cool, damp stone, guiding herself forward through the narrow passage. The tunnels beneath the city were not new to her. She had studied them before, read the theories, debated their origins in academic circles where men in suits laughed at the very idea that a people in exile might have left behind secret roads home.

But now, as she walked those very roads, she realized how little she had truly known.

The Obscured had come for her tonight. They had shut down the conference, blacked out the world's ability to witness what she had revealed, and erased every trace of her research from the university's system. But they could not erase what was written in the bones of the scattered ones. They could not erase her.

Amina slowed her steps. She wasn't alone. A breath of movement. A shift in the air. She turned sharply, pressing herself against the wall, her pulse hammering. The tunnel extended in both directions, darkness stretching endlessly ahead and behind. Then—a whisper. In Hebrew.

She swallowed hard, forcing her breathing to remain controlled. The dim glow from her phone cast shadows against the stone, and for a moment, she thought she saw movement. Then, from the darkness, a voice—soft, aged, carrying the weight of years.

"Dr. Bediako."

Amina's spine went rigid. Her name. Not 'Miss.' Not 'Professor.' But her name. She squinted into the gloom, her grip tightening on her satchel, as if the knowledge inside it still held weight. A figure stepped forward, emerging from the darkness with deliberate slowness, as though materializing from the very bones of the earth itself. A man. Old, but not fragile. His beard, long and silver, brushed against the front of his robes. His face was weathered, his deep-set eyes sharp with something ancient. Not just wisdom—understanding.

Amina inhaled, her mind racing. **"Who are you?"** she asked, her voice steadier than she expected.

The old man studied her, as if considering the right answer. Then, with a small, knowing smile, he spoke.

"I am one of the hidden ones."

Amina's breath caught. Her research had spoken of them in scattered pieces—mentions of an underground network that carried the knowledge of a people in exile, a lineage too dangerous to be recorded in mainstream history. Yet, standing before her was proof that the Hidden Ones were real. She steadied herself. "What do you want from me?"

The old man regarded her for a moment before he spoke. "The question is, what do *you* want from us?" Amina hesitated. She had come for truth. But was that what the Hidden Ones wanted? Were they protectors of knowledge, or something more?

The old man seemed to read her thoughts. "We have preserved what the world has tried to forget. But some among us believe it is no longer enough to protect. We must reveal."

Amina exhaled. "And the others?"

The old man's gaze darkened. "They would rather we remain in the shadows. To fight in silence, or not at all."

A fracture. A divide within their ranks. Amina knew then that whatever choice she made, it would shift more than just her own fate.

Part Two: The Underground Church

Camden, New Jersey – Pastor Sam Matthews

The old Ford rattled as Sam Matthews took another sharp turn, the streets of Camden stretching before him in fractured glimpses of light and shadow. The engine coughed, protesting against the abuse, but Sam didn't ease up. The black SUVs were still behind him. His knuckles were white against the steering wheel. His breath came in controlled, measured exhales, but beneath the practiced calm, his mind was racing. Where could he go?

The Obscured had shut down his phone. No signal. No contact. No help. The police wouldn't protect him. Some of them were probably part of this. His home? No. They would be waiting. His church? Too obvious. That left him with one place.

The underground church.

As he pulled up to the hidden sanctuary, a figure stepped from the shadows, waiting for him.

Ezekiel Shaw.

A name that still carried weight in the movement, though most assumed he had faded into history. But Sam knew better. He had heard the old stories—how Ezekiel had once run safe houses for freedom fighters, how he had helped organize protests when Camden's streets burned with unrest, how he had watched his friends disappear, one by one. But Ezekiel was not just a relic of the past—he was a soldier who had outlasted every battle waged against him. He carried himself with the weight of a man who had buried too many allies and seen too many betrayals. His eyes, dark and unyielding, held the kind of knowledge that only those who had fought wars without uniforms could understand.

Ezekiel's gaze was sharp, his presence unshaken. "You're late."

Sam exhaled, stepping out of the car. "I didn't think there was anyone left."

Ezekiel smirked, the corner of his mouth twitching just slightly. "There aren't many of us anymore. But we've been waiting."

Sam studied the man before him. There were no wasted movements, no unnecessary words. Ezekiel had spent decades learning the language of survival, and he spoke it fluently. He nodded toward the building. "Come inside, Pastor. We have work to do."

Part Three: The Gathering in Camden

Camden, New Jersey – Miguel Rivera

The road stretched endlessly before him, dark and unforgiving. The city lights of Miami had long since faded into the past, swallowed by miles of highway that carried him further from everything he had known. Miguel sat in the passenger seat of the rusted-out pickup truck, his body aching from the last forty-eight hours of running, fighting, and bleeding. Franklin drove in silence, his hands steady on the wheel, his eyes fixed on the road ahead. Rosa was in the backseat, half-asleep, her head resting against the cool glass of the window. No one spoke. There wasn't much left to say. Miami was gone.

They had barely made it onto the boat before the masked men closed in. Whoever they were, they weren't local. They weren't just coming after a group of activists. They were eliminating everyone connected to the truth.

Miguel exhaled slowly, his fingers tightening around the phone in his lap. The message was still there, glowing in the dim light of the truck's dashboard.

Unknown Number: "Sam is waiting."

It had come through when he was still on the water. No number. No trace. But something about it felt deliberate.

It wasn't a warning.

Final Exodus – Part Two   Nacovin J. Norman

It was a call.

Chapter Four: The First Assembly

The Underground Awakens

Part One: The Gathering of Exiles

Camden, New Jersey – The Underground Church

The room carried the weight of history.

Sam Matthews had sat in many churches, but this was something different. It wasn't just a place of worship. It was a war room. A sanctuary for the displaced. A stronghold built for those who had refused to be erased.

Miguel sat across from him, his arms folded, his face still bruised from the battle in Miami. Rosa was beside him, her eyes sharp, scanning everything, not trusting anything. Franklin leaned against the wall, the years of running visible in his worn expression.

And then there was the old man—Ezekiel Shaw.

Sam had heard the name before. His father had mentioned him once in hushed tones, a relic of a time when men like Malcolm and Martin had sat in back rooms like this, deciding the fate of a people.

But Ezekiel wasn't just a relic.

He was still alive.

His eyes, dark and unyielding, swept across the room before finally settling on Sam. "You've got questions," he said.

Sam exhaled. "Yeah."

Ezekiel nodded slowly, as if expecting that answer. He stepped forward, his hands clasped behind his back, his voice steady. "This war didn't start yesterday," he said. "Didn't start with your father. Didn't start with me."

He turned, looking at the bookshelf that lined the back wall—filled with books no university would dare teach. "This war is older than America. Older than Rome. Older than Babylon."

He let that sink in.

Miguel shifted. "What war?"

Ezekiel's lips pressed into a thin line. "The war over who we are."

Silence.

Sam felt something tighten in his chest.

Ezekiel stepped toward one of the bookshelves and ran his fingers over the spines. The air smelled of dust, ink, and oil, like an old temple that had never been abandoned.

He pulled a book from the shelf and turned back to them. The cover was worn, the gold lettering faded. It was a Bible—but not in English.

"This is the Septuagint," he said.

Miguel frowned. "That's the Greek Old Testament, right?"

Ezekiel nodded. "It's the earliest translation we have of the Hebrew scriptures. And the closer you get to the original text, the harder it becomes to deny the truth."

He let the words settle before he continued. "In this version, there's something… different about some of the prophecies. Something that was altered in later translations." He opened the book, turning the pages carefully before stopping at a passage. He handed it to Sam.

Sam looked down, scanning the text.

"And thou, O tower of the flock, cloud of the daughter of Sion, to thee has come, and has entered in, even the first dominion; the kingdom of Babylon shall come to the daughter of Jerusalem." (Micah 4:8, LXX)

Sam's brows furrowed. "What's this supposed to mean?"

Ezekiel sat down across from him. "It means that Jerusalem's children would be carried into Babylon. And later, Babylon would carry them even further."

Franklin spoke up, his voice low. "Into the ships."

The room went still.

Rosa stiffened. Miguel's eyes darkened. Sam felt his pulse slow.

Ezekiel leaned forward, his gaze locked on Sam. "You ever wondered why the slave trade focused on a very specific people? Why they weren't just taking any Africans but were targeting kingdoms like Judah, Ashanti, Yoruba—people who traced their lineage back to David, Solomon, and beyond?"

Sam's throat went dry.

Ezekiel's voice lowered, heavy with something ancient. "They didn't just take slaves." His gaze was unflinching. "They took Israel."

The Disruption of History

Miguel let out a breath, shaking his head. "This sounds like a stretch."

Ezekiel gave him a knowing smile. "Of course it does. That's the point. They made it sound ridiculous so you'd never believe it."

Miguel leaned back, arms crossed. "Even if that were true—why erase it?"

Ezekiel's eyes darkened. "Because a people without a name... are a people without power."

Sam swallowed, staring at the pages before him.

It made too much sense.

The forced conversions, the erasure of indigenous languages, the destruction of entire libraries across Africa, the Christianization of the slaves while stripping them of the text's historical context.

All of it had been deliberate.

Miguel exhaled, rubbing his temples. "So what? You're saying we're all... what, Israelites?"

Ezekiel nodded once. "And that's why they fear the awakening."

A cold chill settled over the room.

Sam had spent his entire life preaching the Bible—but he had never seen it like this. Never been forced to consider the implications. He had always been told that African Americans were simply descendants of random African tribes, victims of a cruel and unfortunate history.

But if they were more than that...

If they were the scattered remnant of something older, something prophetic...

That changed everything.

Rosa cleared her throat, her voice tight. "Let's say you're right. Let's say this is the truth." She gestured around the room. "What does this have to do with us running for our lives?"

Ezekiel leaned back in his chair. "Because the world isn't built for the truth."

Franklin nodded grimly. "We're up against something bigger than governments, bigger than politics. This is a system that's been in place for centuries."

Ezekiel turned to Sam. "Your father knew this. That's why they came for him. It's why they're coming for you now."

Sam's hands tightened. "So what do we do?"

Ezekiel's voice was calm, but unyielding. "We do what the prophets did." He gestured to the book in Sam's hands. "We gather the lost."

Miguel scoffed. "And then what?"

Ezekiel's gaze didn't waver. "We prepare for war."

Part Two: The Obscured's Next Move

Location Unknown – The Council of Control

The Council of Control chamber was as sterile as it was secretive. A long, polished table stood at the room's center, surrounded by men and women who had spent their careers operating in the shadows. This was power—real power. Governments changed, economies collapsed, nations fell, but The Obscured remained.

At the head of the table sat Adrian Solis, his fingers drumming lightly against the armrest of his chair. The screen before him flickered, displaying the latest intelligence reports, heat maps of rising social unrest, and video snippets of underground gatherings across the globe. A small, clipped photo rested at the top of the pile—Samuel Matthews.

He leaned forward. "Tell me," he said smoothly, "how does a small-time pastor from Camden become a priority for our organization?"

Gregory Langston, a former intelligence operative, adjusted his glasses before speaking. "Matthews is more than a pastor. His father was a conduit in the underground network. We assumed those movements had died with the previous generation, but they haven't."

A woman at the far end of the table, Amara Bishop, leaned back in her chair. "Not all of us agree on the methodology being proposed here."

Adrian smirked slightly. "Ah. And so the council reveals its fractures."

Amara's voice remained calm. "Containment and discrediting are one thing. But targeted eradication? Entire families? That's a dangerous precedent."

Adrian's gaze sharpened. "Weakness disguised as morality. This is not a debate, Amara."

Another council member, an older man named Carter Reeves, exhaled heavily. "We've spent centuries mastering control. The best way to ensure a movement never takes root is to make it unbelievable. A well-placed scandal. A fabricated exposé. Turn their prophets into frauds. Their followers into radicals. That's the game we play."

Langston nodded in agreement. "We've manipulated history before. Why not do it again?"

Adrian's fingers stopped drumming. "Because this is different." He gestured toward the list of names on the screen. "They aren't just reclaiming a history—they're mobilizing. They are embedding identity into resistance."

A pause.

Then Amara spoke again. "And killing children? Is that what we've become?"

The silence in the room was heavy.

Adrian glanced at the list again. His expression never wavered, but there was a flicker of calculation in his eyes. "We deploy our assets."

Langston hesitated. "Do we have authorization?"

Adrian leaned back. "Langston. We are the authorization."

He stood, straightening his cuffs, exuding a quiet, deliberate menace. "It's time they understand." He glanced at the screen one last time before walking out.

The last thing he said before the door shut behind him:

"No one escapes history."

Part Three: The Warning

Camden, New Jersey – Denise & Marcus Matthews

Denise hadn't slept.

The clock on the wall read 2:47 AM, but time felt meaningless. The house was dark, the only light coming from the dim glow of the streetlamp outside. She sat in the kitchen, a lukewarm cup of coffee in her hands, staring blankly at the table.

She kept replaying the encounter with the suited man at the door.

Something in his voice had rattled her—not his words, but the confidence behind them. The kind of confidence that came from knowing something she didn't.

She glanced at her phone. Still no messages. No call from Sam.

She exhaled sharply, rubbing her temples. Where was he?

A creak on the stairs made her tense.

Marcus appeared at the doorway, still in his T-shirt and basketball shorts, his height casting a long shadow against the kitchen tile.

"You're still up?" he asked.

Denise managed a small smile. "You're still up."

Marcus shrugged, stepping inside. He hesitated, then grabbed a glass from the cabinet and poured himself some water. He didn't sit, just leaned against the counter, watching her.

Something in his posture told her he knew.

He wasn't a little boy anymore. He was thirteen, taller than his father, strong, sharp. He could feel the weight of the moment even if no one told him what was going on.

So she told him.

"At your father's church, he's been talking about something... something bigger than us." She swallowed. "History. Identity. The way things have been covered up for centuries."

Marcus frowned. "Covered up?"

Denise nodded. "There are people who don't want those things uncovered."

Marcus studied her, his mind working. "You mean, like, government stuff?"

Denise shook her head. "Bigger than that."

Marcus leaned forward, gripping the counter. "Mom, are you saying Dad's in trouble because of—"

Knock. Knock. Knock.

They both froze.

Denise's heart lurched into her throat.

Marcus glanced toward the front door, then back at her. Not again.

She stood slowly, motioning for him to stay put. Her pulse roared in her ears as she approached the door, her fingers trembling as she peered through the peephole.

She barely recognized what she saw.

A woman stood there, breathless, glancing over her shoulder as if being followed. Her hair was disheveled, her clothes wrinkled, and she was gripping something tight against her chest.

It took Denise a second to realize—it was a child.

She unlocked the door and cracked it open.

The woman's face was filled with panic.

"Denise Matthews?" she whispered.

Denise stiffened. "Who are you?"

The woman swallowed hard. "Your husband sent me."

The Arrival of a Fugitive

Denise hesitated only for a moment before pulling the woman inside and shutting the door.

Marcus stepped forward cautiously, eyeing the woman and the small child she carried.

Denise spoke first. "Start talking."

Part Four: The Fugitive's Story

Camden, New Jersey – The Matthews Home

Denise stared at the woman now standing in her living room, the child clutched tightly in her arms. The woman's breathing was uneven, her hands trembling as she glanced at the door behind her, as if expecting it to be broken down at any moment.

Marcus stood near the kitchen, silent but alert. He had stopped questioning what was happening and was now just watching, absorbing every detail.

Denise took a slow step forward. "Who are you?" she asked again, this time more firmly.

The woman swallowed hard. "My name is Naomi." She shifted the child in her arms, a small boy no older than four. His eyes were wide, round, scanning the room with confusion but not fear. "Your husband sent me."

Denise's pulse jumped. "Sam? Where is he? Is he alright?"

Naomi shook her head quickly. "I don't know. He told me to find you. He said if I ever had nowhere else to go, you would understand."

Denise frowned. "Understand what?"

Naomi's lips parted slightly, but no words came out at first. Then, after a deep breath, she whispered, "They're killing us."

A long silence followed.

Denise exhaled sharply. "Who?"

Naomi hesitated, as if saying it out loud would make it even more real. "The same people who are after your husband. The same ones who erased entire families from history. They've been hunting us for centuries. And now... now they know we're waking up."

Marcus shifted slightly. "Waking up to what?"

Naomi turned her gaze to him. "The truth."

Denise swallowed hard, her mind racing. She thought about the man who had come to the house earlier that day, the way he had spoken, the way he had studied her, as if already deciding her fate. Sam had been warning her for years that something deeper was at play. That history itself had been rewritten to bury their identity. She had believed him... but now, for the first time, she **felt** it.

She looked back at Naomi, her expression steel. "You and the boy can stay here for now. But I need to know everything. From the beginning."

Naomi nodded, her shoulders relaxing slightly as she finally took a seat. "Then you need to understand who I am."

Part Five: The Exodus Before the Exodus

Naomi sat on the couch, adjusting the blanket around her son as he finally dozed off against her shoulder. She looked exhausted but determined, as if she had rehearsed this moment in her mind a hundred times. When she finally spoke, her voice was steady but laced with sorrow.

"My family is from Ethiopia," she began. "My grandmother always told us stories of who we were before we were scattered. She would talk about how we were forced to leave Jerusalem long before the Romans ever burned the temple. How we carried our traditions with us, keeping them hidden so that one day we would remember."

Denise listened carefully, glancing at Marcus, who was hanging onto every word.

Naomi continued, "My grandmother used to say, 'We did not forget who we were. They made us forget.' And for a long time, I didn't understand what she meant. Not until I started researching it myself. Not until I realized that history—the history we are taught—is a weapon."

Marcus frowned. "A weapon?"

Naomi nodded. "Because if you control what people believe about themselves, you control how they see the world. How they see each other. And most importantly—how they see their enemies."

Denise inhaled sharply. "And the people after you? After Sam? They want to keep that control."

"They have to," Naomi said. "Because if we wake up, we don't just challenge their power. We undo it."

The words sat heavy in the air. Marcus shifted uncomfortably, as if he was only now realizing just how deep this went.

Denise cleared her throat. "And what about now? Why did Sam send you here?"

Naomi swallowed. "Because they found me."

Denise's stomach clenched. "You mean—"

"The Obscured." Naomi's hands gripped the blanket over her child, her knuckles white. "They know who I am. They've been watching for years, but I always stayed ahead. Until last night. They came for me in the middle of the night. My husband..." She broke off, her voice shaking. "He didn't make it."

Denise reached forward instinctively, placing a hand on Naomi's arm. "I'm so sorry."

Naomi inhaled, forcing herself to continue. "Sam knew. He told me they'd come. He told me that if I had to run, I should come here. That you would protect my son."

Denise's jaw tightened. She had spent years trying to stay in the background, keeping her son out of whatever battle Sam was always fighting. But now the battle had come to her doorstep.

She turned to Marcus, who was staring at Naomi in silent understanding. He wasn't a child anymore. He had seen the way the world worked. And now, he was seeing **why** it worked that way.

"What do we do?" Marcus asked quietly.

Denise exhaled. "We keep moving. We stay ahead of them."

Naomi looked up. "I have a contact. Someone who can get us out of Camden, at least for now. But we have to go soon."

Denise nodded, already standing. "Then we go."

Marcus frowned. "And Dad?"

Denise hesitated for only a second before answering. "We find him. And we bring him back."

Part Six: The Obscured's Strike

Location Unknown – Council of Control

Adrian Solis stood in front of the illuminated map, his expression unreadable as he observed the movements of their assets.

"Matthews has gone dark," Langston reported. "But we still have surveillance on the house. The wife and son are still inside. We're waiting for your orders."

Adrian tapped a finger against his chin. "And the Ethiopian girl?"

"She made contact with them," Langston confirmed. "They're together now."

A slow smile spread across Adrian's face. "Good. That means we don't have to find Matthews to break him."

Langston shifted uncomfortably. "Are we escalating?"

Adrian turned, his smile still in place but his eyes cold. "We've played the game long enough, Langston. They need a reminder of what happens when you challenge the narrative."

Langston hesitated, then exhaled. "Understood. I'll have the strike team move in tonight."

Adrian nodded, but his gaze lingered on the names on the screen. Sam Matthews. Denise Matthews. Marcus Matthews. Naomi Solomon.

History had been rewritten before.

And tonight, he would make sure it stayed that way.

Chapter Five: The Awakening and the Cost

Part One: The Shadow of Deception

The silence inside the safehouse felt unnatural. Not the kind that brought peace, but the kind that warned of something inevitable. Naomi sat in the farthest corner, her arms wrapped tightly around the small child in her lap. The boy, no older than four, clung to her, his tiny fingers knotted into the fabric of her sweater. She had been like this since they arrived, barely speaking, barely moving, as if afraid that the very act of breathing too loudly would expose them to whatever horrors she had already seen.

The others didn't press her for details yet. They were still trying to catch their own breath. The escape from Camden had been brutal—a chase through the skeletal remains of a city gutted by corruption and war. They had slipped through alleyways, dodged surveillance, and crossed the border into the safehouse on the other side, but it never felt far enough. The danger wasn't just behind them—it was woven into the very air they breathed.

Miguel stood near the doorway, his gun still in his hand, not gripping it as if he were ready to fire but also not prepared to put it down. His face, hard-edged with exhaustion and frustration, remained fixed on the screen of his encrypted phone. Each second brought new messages, new confirmations of what was happening across the world.

Sam Matthews paced the length of the room, his mind working through the reality that had just been dropped into their laps. The war had escalated, and they were out of time. Denise sat beside Marcus, her fingers tightening around his as if to reassure herself that he was still there. That her son hadn't been stolen away like so many others.

Ezekiel Shaw, standing with his back against the wall, folded his arms, his aged but sharp eyes scanning the room. He had seen war before. And now, he was seeing it again.

Naomi finally spoke, her voice barely above a whisper but cutting through the heavy silence like a blade. "Everyone's dead."

Sam stopped pacing.

Naomi didn't look up. "The people I was with… my family. My entire cell. They're gone." Her voice cracked on the last word, and she sucked in a sharp breath, forcing it down. "We were careful. We weren't sloppy. But it didn't matter."

Miguel exhaled sharply, locking his phone. "That's because they already knew where to find you."

Naomi lifted her head, her tear-streaked face filled with something between rage and hopelessness. "How? We took every precaution."

Ezekiel pushed off the wall, stepping forward. "Because this was never just about silencing people. It's about erasing them."

Naomi blinked. "What?"

Miguel unlocked his phone and turned the screen toward her. The headline burned into their minds like an open wound:

"Thousands of Believers Gone Without a Trace—Is This the Rapture?"

Naomi's breath hitched. Denise's grip on Marcus tightened. Sam moved closer, his expression dark.

"They're making it look like prophecy," he muttered.

A beat of silence.

Ezekiel spoke first, his voice calm but unyielding. "They're using the rapture doctrine to justify mass exterminations." He crossed the room, grabbing a tattered Bible from the pile of belongings stacked against the wall. The pages were worn, written in, highlighted by countless hands over the years. He flipped quickly, stopping at Matthew 24.

"The church has spent decades preaching that believers will disappear before the tribulation," Ezekiel continued, scanning the passage with the ease of a man who had lived through too many deceptions. "But what did Yeshua actually say?"

He read aloud, his voice steady:

"Immediately after the tribulation of those days, the sun shall be darkened, and the moon shall not give her light, and the stars shall fall from heaven, and the powers of the heavens shall be shaken. And then shall appear the sign of the Son of Man in heaven: and then shall all the tribes of the earth mourn, and they shall see the Son of Man coming in the clouds of heaven with power and great glory. And he shall send his angels with a great sound of a trumpet, and they shall gather together his elect from the four winds, from one end of heaven to the other."

A heavy pause.

Naomi's lips parted, but no words came out. Denise shook her head slowly, her voice barely above a whisper. "Wait… after the tribulation?"

Ezekiel nodded. "That's what it says."

Denise sat up straighter, eyes narrowing. "Then why have we been taught something else our whole lives?"

Ezekiel's eyes darkened. "Because a complacent church is a weak one."

Naomi blinked rapidly, as if trying to push the information away. "But this doesn't make sense. If the rapture isn't real, then why are they pushing this narrative?"

Miguel exhaled sharply, flipping to another article. "Because if people think the rapture already happened, they won't fight back."

Naomi let out a shaky breath. "They'll just assume they were never chosen."

Sam's stomach twisted. It was brilliant in its cruelty.

Ezekiel set the Bible down. "This isn't about faith. This is about control. And if they can convince the world that resistance is futile, they don't need to fight us. They just need us to give up."

Miguel clenched his jaw. "Which means we have to move. Now."

Naomi wiped at her face, something shifting in her eyes. She wasn't just grieving anymore. She was processing. Understanding.

She inhaled deeply, steadying herself. "What do you need me to do?"

A shift in the air.

Ezekiel nodded approvingly. "Good question."

Miguel turned back to his phone, fingers flying across the screen. "I need to contact our people in Ghana, Brazil, Haiti—anywhere this message hasn't reached yet. If they haven't started purging those areas, we might still have a chance."

Sam turned to Naomi. "You said your group was taken—were you able to salvage anything before you ran?"

Naomi hesitated. Then, slowly, she reached into her bag and pulled out a small hard drive.

Miguel's gaze sharpened. "What's on it?"

Naomi exhaled. "Everything. Names, movements, hidden safehouses, funding channels." She swallowed hard. "But more than that... I think I have proof that this isn't just a cover-up. They've been planning this for decades."

Sam's pulse quickened. "How much proof?"

Naomi held the drive up. Miguel took it carefully, staring down at the small device as if it held the fate of the entire war inside.

"Enough to burn the whole system down."

Part Two: The Sermon That Shook the World

The safehouse had never felt smaller.

The walls, once a shield against the outside world, now seemed to close in, suffocating under the weight of what they were about to do. This wasn't just about survival anymore. This was war. Not fought with bullets or bombs—but with truth.

Miguel sat at the long wooden table, assembling their broadcast setup with the precision of a soldier preparing his weapon before battle. Naomi stood beside him, eyes darting between lines of code and security feeds. Every keystroke brought them closer to the moment when they would lift the veil, when they would expose the greatest deception of modern history.

Sam Matthews stood near the doorway, watching, waiting. Praying.

Denise sat with Marcus, holding him close, as if the strength of her embrace could shield him from the war about to be unleashed. Ezekiel Shaw sat in the corner, arms folded, watching, his old eyes heavy with knowledge. With understanding.

"You realize what you're about to do?" Ezekiel asked, his voice calm but weighted.

Miguel didn't look up from the screen. "Yeah. We're about to expose a genocide."

Ezekiel nodded. "And you think they'll let you?"

Sam exhaled sharply. "They won't."

Ezekiel leaned forward, resting his hands on his cane. "Then I hope you're ready for what comes next."

Naomi gave a sharp nod. "You're live in three… two… one."

The camera flickered to life.

Sam's face filled the screen, worn yet resolute. His eyes, dark with conviction, locked onto an audience he could not see but whose presence he could feel— scattered across the world, in hidden rooms, behind closed doors, in places where truth had been exiled. And yet, they were watching. They were listening.

And so he began.

"To those with ears to hear, listen.

To those who have been scattered, remember.

To those who have been blinded, see.

"The world has lied to you. It has told you that you are nothing. That your history is lost. That your people are cursed, abandoned, broken beyond repair. That you are a shadow in someone else's story, that your past is a burden and your future a chain.

"But I tell you today—the reckoning has come.

"The book of Deuteronomy told us long ago:

'And the Lord shall scatter thee among all people, from one end of the earth even unto the other… and there thou shalt serve other gods, which neither thou nor thy fathers have known, even wood and stone.' (Deut. 28:64, LXX)

"The prophecy was clear. We were scattered. We were enslaved. We were renamed, rewritten, and reduced to property. But they never intended for us to wake up. They never thought we would remember.

"But we have.

"The time of awakening is here. The time of rising is now. They branded you as slaves. They erased your names, stole your inheritance, rewrote your lineage, and fed you their history. They called you lost. But the Most High has declared—you were never lost. You were hidden.

"They co-opted your language. Took words like 'woke'—which once meant awakening—and turned it into a weapon against you. They hijacked your music, your culture, your inventions, while telling you that you contributed nothing. They erased your history while celebrating the fruits of your labor under a different name. They gave you false doctrines, twisted scripture, and told you to wait for an escape—a rapture that was never written—while they continued their plundering.

"Look at what they attack. DEI. Affirmative Action. Black History. Critical Race Theory. Reparations. They fear anything that reminds you of who you are or restores you to what you once were. They brand truth as controversy and justice as terrorism. They silence you because they know—if you wake up, the prophecy is fulfilled.

"Do you not see the pattern? They enslaved you, then called you free. They stole your inventions, then erased your name. They slaughtered you, then told you to forget. They made laws against your people, then blamed you for the chains. They built their institutions on your back, then told you to pull yourself up.

"And when you started to rise, they moved the goalpost. They called you ungrateful. They said 'that was in the past.' They told you to move on while still reaping the benefits of what was taken.

"They feared the civil rights movement, so they made it a chapter in a textbook. They feared Malcolm and Martin, so they reduced them to soundbites. They feared your unity, so they flooded your communities with drugs, with guns, with policies designed to shackle you without chains.

"And now, when you begin to remember, when you begin to reclaim, they panic. They call you radical. They say you are trying to rewrite history. But history was already rewritten—by them.

"The book of Baruch tells us,

'I will bring them again into the land which I promised with an oath unto their fathers, Abraham, Isaac, and Jacob, and they shall be lords of it.' (Baruch 2:34, LXX)

"This is not about rebellion. This is not about revenge. This is about truth. And the truth is this— the kingdoms of this world have thrived on the blood of the scattered ones. They have built their empires on stolen backs and broken promises. They have rewritten history to bury the bones of a people whose presence threatens their lies.

"But now the bones are rattling. The breath of life is stirring. The valley of dry bones is rising, and no amount of deception, censorship, or force can stop it.

"The Messiah himself said:

'Ye shall know the truth, and the truth shall make you free.' (John 8:32)

"But freedom is dangerous to those who rule by deception. Freedom is a death sentence to empires built on lies. That is why they fear this message. That is why they silence us. That is why they kill those who dare to speak.

"But their time is up.

"You are not the minority. You are not the cursed. You are the inheritance of the Most High. You are the children of Zion. And now, the time has come to remember who you are.

"The world calls this extremism. They call it conspiracy. They will call me a radical. A terrorist. A threat.

"And they are right.

"I am a threat. Not to peace, but to deception. Not to life, but to the lies that have strangled it. I am dangerous to the wicked because I will no longer be silent.

"And neither will you.

"The final exodus has begun. The time of captivity is ending. And the rulers of this world know it.

"To those who are listening—wake up. Shake off the dust. The war for truth has already begun. And silence is no longer an option.

"Let the watchers hear. Let the wicked tremble.

"Because the reckoning is here."

The screen flickered.

A sharp crack split the silence.

Gunfire.

Miguel moved first, slamming the laptop shut as Naomi yanked the cords free. The room erupted into chaos. They had been found.

The war was no longer coming.

It was here.

Chapter Six: Into the Unknown

Part One: A World on the Brink

The night air was damp with the scent of rain and rusted steel. Sam Matthews moved through the abandoned rail yard with careful precision, every step deliberate, every breath measured. The ground beneath his boots crunched softly, the scattered gravel shifting as he signaled Denise and Marcus forward.

Marcus was taller than both his mother and father, his athletic frame moving with the quiet discipline of someone who had learned—too young—that survival required strategy. His movements mirrored Sam's: low, calculated, ready.

Denise's breathing was controlled, but Sam could feel the tension radiating from her. He didn't blame her. None of this was supposed to happen.

Miguel was ahead, crouched near an old control tower, his silhouette barely distinguishable in the darkness. His right hand rested on the grip of his pistol, his body taut with the anticipation of violence. When he turned toward Sam, his expression was unreadable.

"They're here." Miguel's voice was low, clipped. "Moving slow. Three—maybe four."

Denise stiffened. "How close?"

Miguel glanced past her, then back at Sam. "Close enough."

Sam exhaled through his nose, adjusting the strap of his backpack. This was coming, whether they were ready or not.

For days, **The Obscured** had been tightening their grip, flooding the world with misinformation, framing him as a radical, a criminal, a terrorist. He had expected the character assassination, but when it wasn't enough to bury him, when the people kept listening, The Obscured escalated.

Now, they weren't just erasing him.

They were hunting him.

A faint sound echoed from the east side of the yard—a careful footstep.

Sam shifted, his eyes narrowing toward the source. Miguel was right. They were moving in slow, controlled. **Professionals.**

Sam weighed the options: ✓ **They could run.** But there was no guarantee they wouldn't be seen before reaching the SUV. ✓ **They could hide.** But The Obscured's tactical teams weren't the kind to leave empty-handed. ✓ **Or they could make the first move.**

Sam met Miguel's gaze. The other man didn't speak, but he didn't have to. The decision was made.

Miguel moved first.

He reached down, grabbed a rusted pipe from the ground, and hurled it toward a stack of old freight crates. The metal clanged against the steel containers with a loud bang, the sound reverberating through the yard.

Immediately, voices snapped to attention.

"There—movement!"

Sam grabbed Denise's wrist. "Go. Now."

She didn't hesitate.

Marcus was already moving, his strides quick but quiet as he slipped between two rows of storage units. Denise followed, keeping pace despite the tension that coiled in her frame.

Sam moved last, his heartbeat steady as he maneuvered behind a set of derailed train cars.

Miguel's distraction had worked. **The Obscured's team had shifted toward the sound, their weapons angled, their communication sharp.**

But it wouldn't take long for them to realize the trick.

They had seconds.

Miguel was already waiting by the SUV, his hand gripping the door handle. As soon as Marcus slid into the back seat, Denise following close behind, Sam reached for the passenger-side door—

And the first gunshot rang out.

Denise gasped, instinctively shielding Marcus. Miguel slammed the accelerator, throwing the SUV forward just as another shot whizzed past the side mirror.

Sam twisted, his pulse spiking. The gunfire wasn't targeted—not yet. The Obscured's team didn't want to kill them before confirming the job. **They wanted to capture them.**

Miguel took a sharp turn onto an open service road, tires screeching against wet pavement. Sam's body rocked with the motion, but he barely registered it. His mind was racing ahead, running through the next move.

"Where?" Miguel barked, one hand gripping the wheel, the other reaching for the secondary firearm strapped under his seat.

Sam clenched his jaw. "The safehouse is compromised."

Denise turned in her seat, her expression tense. "Then where do we go?"

For a moment, the only sound was the roar of the engine, the city's skyline stretching into the distance like the edge of a battlefield.

Sam exhaled, his grip tightening on the dashboard.

"There's only one place left."

Miguel's fingers flexed on the wheel. "Don't say it."

Sam met his gaze. **"Jerusalem."**

Miguel cursed under his breath. "That's suicide."

"No." Sam shook his head. **"That's where this started. And that's where it ends."**

The SUV barreled down the empty road, the weight of fate pressing against them.

The world was on the edge of revelation.

And the war had only just begun.

Part Two: The Flight into Hostile Skies

The moment the wheels lifted off the runway, Sam knew something was wrong.

The air should have felt lighter. The tension should have ebbed just a little, even for a second. But instead, it thickened. **Naomi shifted in her seat beside him, one hand pressing against her side. The makeshift bandage Miguel had wrapped around her before they boarded was already showing signs of red.**

Marcus noticed first. His brow furrowed, his gaze flicking between Naomi's pale face and Sam's tense expression. "She's bleeding through."

Denise turned sharply, her voice taut. "We need better medical supplies. Now."

Miguel was already digging into the emergency kit stored under the seat. "We've got gauze, antiseptic, but no painkillers strong enough for this."

Sam pressed a hand against his temple. They weren't even in international airspace yet, and the situation was already deteriorating.

A soft chime echoed through the cabin, followed by the pilot's voice.

"Ladies and gentlemen, we have an unexpected issue with airspace clearance. We're being advised to adjust course by air traffic control."

Sam's stomach twisted. **Adjust course?**

Miguel's eyes narrowed. "That's not normal."

Denise exhaled sharply. "They're trying to reroute us."

Sam nodded grimly. "The Obscured isn't waiting until we land."

Marcus, still watching Naomi, whispered, "So what do we do?"

Sam turned toward Miguel. The other man was already checking his firearm, jaw set. **"We prepare for turbulence. And not the kind the pilot warns you about."**

Chapter Seven: The War Goes Public

Part One: Shadows Over Jerusalem

The jet's wheels had barely met the tarmac before Sam felt it.

Something in the air had changed.

The sense of unease that had clung to him since they left American airspace had not faded. If anything, it had sharpened, pressing against his ribs like a silent warning. The flight had been tense—too tense. Naomi had been in and out of consciousness, her body weakened by the wound that still needed proper medical attention. Miguel had barely spoken, his focus split between watching the skies and checking his sidearm. Denise had held it together, but Sam could see the weight in her eyes. And Marcus—

His son had watched everything.

The boy had barely said a word since they left, but Sam had caught him studying the others. Watching their movements, reading their expressions, absorbing every unspoken detail like a soldier learning the battlefield. It unsettled him, but he also knew Marcus wasn't wrong.

They weren't safe. Not here. Not anywhere.

The distant glow of fire smudged the horizon, sending thin plumes of smoke curling into the dark sky. Helicopters hovered over the Old City, their blinking red lights flickering like unnatural stars. The streets below, lined with ancient stone and modern asphalt, pulsed with movement—crowds spilling into alleyways, barricades forming, voices rising in anger and defiance.

Jerusalem was not at peace.

And neither were they.

Sam unbuckled his seatbelt slowly, inhaling through his nose, exhaling just as steadily. His fingers curled around the edge of the seat. This was it.

Naomi stirred beside him, her breath uneven. Denise shifted immediately, adjusting the makeshift bandage wrapped around her abdomen. Naomi winced but waved Denise off weakly.

"I'm good."

"No, you're not," Denise muttered. "And we still don't know where we're taking you."

"We'll figure it out," Sam said, but even as the words left his mouth, he knew it was a lie. They had no plan. No sanctuary waiting. The only thing ahead of them was a city already on the edge of chaos.

Miguel checked his gun for the third time. "We need to move before they know we're here."

Sam nodded. "Time to move."

The Prophecy and the Battle for Truth

As the jet doors opened and the heat of the Jerusalem night pressed against them, Sam's mind echoed with scripture. The Septuagint had foretold this—had warned of a time when the nations would conspire against the truth.

"Why do the nations rage, and the peoples plot in vain? The kings of the earth set themselves, and the rulers take counsel together, against the Lord and against His anointed..." (Psalm 2:1-2, Septuagint).

The Obscured knew prophecy better than most. That was why they manipulated it. Controlled it. Turned it into a weapon of mass deception. The destruction of the Dome, the orchestrated chaos—this wasn't just politics. This was a manufactured war against the awakening of a people long suppressed.

Sam knew it. And now the world was starting to see it, too.

The Contact – A Road Without a Destination

The man waiting for them just beyond the tarmac was older, his features carved from long years of study and silence. Professor Daniel Rafiq.

Historian. Scholar. A man who had spent a lifetime walking the blurred line between truth and survival.

As soon as they reached him, he wasted no time.

"You shouldn't have come here," he said, voice low.

Sam met his gaze. "We didn't have a choice."

Rafiq exhaled through his nose, glancing toward the dark streets stretching beyond the airport. His face was unreadable, but his posture was rigid, his fingers twitching at his sides.

Miguel noticed it first. "You're nervous."

Rafiq didn't deny it. "I agreed to this meeting because I believe in truth. But truth is a dangerous thing in a city built on old wounds." His eyes flicked toward Sam. "You've reopened them."

Sam's jaw tightened.

"They were never closed."

Rafiq studied him for a long moment. Then, reluctantly, he nodded. "Come."

The black SUV waiting for them was unmarked, the kind governments used when they wanted to watch without being seen. Rafiq opened the back door, gesturing for them to get in.

Denise hesitated. "Where are we going?"

Rafiq didn't answer right away.

Then, softly—

"To the one place where truth still whispers."

Final Exodus – Part Two   Nacovin J. Norman

The City is on Fire

As they drove through the city, the streets swelled with unrest.

Crowds gathered in tight knots, their voices raised in anger, in demand. Some carried signs in Hebrew, Arabic, and English—some in languages Sam couldn't immediately recognize. Their meaning, however, was clear.

We remember.

We will not be erased.

Who are the chosen?

Miguel let out a low whistle, shaking his head. "It's everywhere."

Naomi had pulled up a live feed on her tablet, her face illuminated by the glow of the screen. "It's not just here," she murmured. "It's spreading."

She turned the screen toward them. Footage from Brazil. From Ghana. From the U.S. From London.

In city after city, people were rising.

Demanding answers.

And The Obscured was scrambling to stop them.

Denise exhaled. "This isn't just about us anymore."

"No," Sam murmured. His gaze darkened. "It never was."

Marcus, who had remained quiet until now, finally spoke. "They're waiting for someone to tell them what happens next."

His voice was quiet but steady. Sam turned slightly, watching his son.

Marcus's fingers tapped lightly against the window, his eyes scanning the crowd. "They don't have a leader yet. Just energy."

Sam didn't answer, but the words sat heavy between them.

Miguel muttered under his breath. "Then we better move before they pick the wrong one."

The Obscured Tighten the Noose

From a darkened command center, Ross watched the live feeds with cold detachment. The city was already burning, but soon, they would take control of the flames.

An agent approached cautiously, his posture tense. "Sir, Matthews and his group have landed. They're in transit with Professor Rafiq."

Ross exhaled slowly, his fingers tapping against the steel armrest of his chair. "What's our play?"

"The council wants a quiet extraction," the agent said, shifting slightly under Ross's gaze. "No public spectacle. No unnecessary noise."

Ross's lips curled into something that might have been a smirk, but it carried no warmth. "A martyr is only useful if there's something left to remember."

He leaned forward, eyes cold. "Prepare the kill teams."

Chapter Eight: The Fall of Empires

Part One: Smoke and Ruin

Jerusalem had always been a battleground. Not just of nations or armies, but of ideas, of faiths, of histories woven together like strands of an unbreakable tapestry. Empires had come and gone, rulers had carved their names into its stones, and prophets had walked its streets proclaiming truths that had either reshaped civilizations or gotten them killed.

Tonight, the war would change forever.

Smoke drifted through the sky, turning the early morning light into a dull, hazy glow over the city. The scent of burning rubber and charred stone filled the air, thick enough to choke. Somewhere in the distance, sirens blared, echoing off the ancient walls. Protesters clashed with riot police in the streets, their voices rising in anger, in desperation, in something that could no longer be contained.

Sam Matthews crouched behind a half-destroyed market stall, his breath coming in ragged pulls as he scanned the chaos unfolding before him. His body ached from the sprint through the city, but there was no time to slow down. They were being hunted.

Denise pressed herself against a nearby stone pillar, her arm wrapped protectively around Marcus, who had grown eerily silent in the last hour. The boy had seen too much already, but there was no shielding him from this. Not anymore.

Miguel was tense, his pistol drawn, his eyes sweeping their surroundings with the cold calculation of a man who had spent too many years dodging death. Naomi, still weak from her injuries, leaned against the remnants of a crumbling wall, her face pale but her grip firm on the tablet she had risked her life for.

Their broadcast had gone global. The truth was out. But the war had just begun.

The Streets Ignite

Hours earlier, they had barely escaped.

The moment Rabbi Levi fell, The Obscured had moved swiftly. Snipers had rained bullets down on the crowd, hoping to eliminate any key figures before the moment turned into a movement. The team had fled through alleyways, weaving through burning wreckage and hastily abandoned checkpoints. The streets had erupted—first in chaos, then in resistance.

Now, there was no doubt.

They weren't just witnesses.

They were targets.

Sam's mind worked rapidly through their options, but there weren't many. They couldn't run forever. Hiding wasn't an option—not anymore. The Obscured had framed them for a terrorist attack, and now, every government in the world was after them.

Denise adjusted the strap on her bag, her voice barely above a whisper. "We need to get off the streets. Every news channel is calling for your head, Sam. It's not just The Obscured anymore—it's the world."

He already knew that.

Every screen they passed flickered with his face, plastered alongside words like **'TERRORIST MASTERMIND,' 'THE MAN WHO SET JERUSALEM ABLAZE,'** and **'GLOBAL THREAT TO RELIGIOUS STABILITY.'** The fabricated reports were seamless, the narrative so airtight that even those who had believed in them yesterday would start to question themselves today.

Miguel's jaw tightened. "It's happening faster than I thought. They didn't just frame us—they already wrote our deaths."

Sam's fists clenched at his sides. This wasn't just about discrediting them anymore. This was about erasing them.

Before he could respond, an explosion tore through the next street over. The force sent a tremor through the ground, shaking dust from the rooftops, rattling the bones of the city. Screams followed.

Miguel ducked lower. "That wasn't random."

No, it wasn't. This was part of the next phase. The Obscured wasn't just making them disappear.

They were burning the world around them.

Ross Regroups – The Empire Cracks

Inside a fortified military compound miles away, Ross stood in front of a wall of screens, his face eerily calm despite the madness unfolding outside.

His operatives were scrambling behind him, shouting over one another as reports flooded in. **The Dome of the Rock had been destroyed. Cities were on fire. The global response was spiraling out of control.**

And the Awakening Movement?

It wasn't crushed.

It was growing.

Ross exhaled, his lips curling into something that wasn't quite a smile.

He had spent his life ensuring that this moment never came.

And yet—here it was.

One of his agents approached hesitantly. "Sir… the international response is escalating. Governments are demanding confirmation—should we proceed with labeling Matthews as a rogue militant?"

Ross barely looked at him. "Of course."

Another operative spoke up, his voice unsteady. "But, sir… what if people don't believe it?"

Ross finally turned to face him, his expression blank. "It doesn't matter if they believe it. It matters if they fear it."

A long pause. Then the agent gave a stiff nod before moving back to his station.

Ross turned back toward the screens, his fingers steepling under his chin.

Everything was unraveling.

But that didn't mean he had lost.

Not yet.

Because there was one move left to make.

He picked up his secure phone, dialing a number he had only called once before.

A pause.

Then—a voice answered.

Ross spoke calmly, as if he were ordering a morning coffee.

"It's time to involve the Vatican."

The People Rise

Back in the city, Sam and his team reached the edges of the riots.

The protests had grown into something more. People weren't just demanding answers anymore. They weren't just holding signs.

They were tearing down the old order.

And at the center of it all, standing atop the steps of the Temple Mount, was **Rabbi Yitzhak Levi.**

Alive.

Sam's breath caught.

The Rabbi's voice rose above the madness, his words cutting through the chaos like a blade. He wasn't trying to calm the people. He wasn't trying to stop the revolution.

He was leading it.

"The time of deception is over!"

"The scattered ones are rising!"

"And the rulers of this world are trembling!"

Sam barely heard Miguel's voice beside him. "Sam, what do we do?"

He didn't answer.

Because in that moment, as he locked eyes with Rabbi Levi, he already knew.

This wasn't about running.

This wasn't about survival.

This was prophecy.

And they were in the middle of it.

Chapter Nine: The Gathering of Nations

Part One: The Summoning of Kings

The world was on fire.

The assassination of Rabbi Levi had not stopped the Awakening—it had ignited it. Protests had erupted into revolts, revolts into uprisings. From Jerusalem to Cairo, from Lagos to Paris, from New York to Mecca, the people were no longer waiting for permission to reclaim what had been stolen.

Governments struggled to contain the unrest, but suppression only fanned the flames. The movement was no longer isolated—it was a global reckoning.

And yet, in the midst of the chaos, something even more dangerous was unfolding.

The world's rulers were gathering.

Not in the open, not for public speeches or political maneuvering. This meeting would not be televised. It would not be discussed on the news. It would be whispered about in conspiracy circles, denounced as fiction even as it shaped the future.

In an underground chamber beneath the Vatican, beyond the marble halls where tourists wandered and where priests still clung to the illusion of righteousness, the true seat of power met in secret.

A long stone table stretched through the center of the chamber, its surface ancient, stained with the weight of centuries of decisions made in darkness. At this table, the rulers of this world had gathered.

A Pope. A Prime Minister. A Sheikh. A General. An Emperor.

And others—men whose names the public would never know, men whose faces were not in history books, but whose influence had shaped the fates of nations.

The room was silent except for the low hum of security machines scanning for surveillance, for leaks, for any crack in the veil of secrecy. The world outside was in freefall, but here, beneath the Vatican, the architects of history prepared their next move.

Finally, one of them spoke.

"This cannot continue," the Prime Minister of Israel said, his voice sharp. "The world is watching. The Awakening Movement is not just an American problem anymore. It is global. And it is out of control."

A Cardinal from the Vatican folded his hands, his expression unreadable. "This is not just a political matter. This is prophecy. And it is unraveling in a way that threatens the very foundations of order."

A Saudi Prince leaned forward, his jaw tight. "The destruction of the Dome of the Rock has already pushed us to the brink. We are one act away from total war."

The Pope, his face hidden in the shadows, finally spoke. His voice was soft. Too soft.

"Then let us not wait for that act to come. Let us create it."

The table fell silent.

The General from China tilted his head slightly. "You are proposing a preemptive war?"

The Pope did not smile, but the weight of his gaze was enough to make even the hardened men in the room uneasy. "No. I am proposing a final war. One that will settle this matter permanently."

A long pause.

Then, the Sheikh of Mecca exhaled slowly, choosing his words carefully. "If we move openly against the Awakening, we risk exposing our own deceptions. Many of my own people are asking questions. The old control is breaking."

The Pope's fingers tapped slowly against the table. "Which is why we must move swiftly. The Awakening must be framed not as a revolution, but as a threat to all faiths. To all nations. To the very fabric of civilization."

The Prime Minister's eyes narrowed. "And how do you propose we do that?"

The Pope's lips barely moved.

"We give them their Messiah."

Ross's Last Play – The False Messiah

Ross sat in his private command center, his face still bruised from the chaos in Jerusalem. His operatives were scrambling, reports flooding in, but he no longer cared about the details. The protests, the broadcasts, the uprisings—none of it mattered anymore.

Because the final move was already in play.

He turned his gaze toward the encrypted file blinking on his screen.

PROJECT REDEMPTION.

Ross leaned back in his chair, exhaling slowly. "It's time."

One of his agents hesitated. "Sir, are you sure? We still don't know if—"

Ross smiled.

"Let the world see its savior."

The agent swallowed hard, then nodded, issuing the final command.

Within moments, the most sophisticated AI-driven broadcast in history began.

Across every major network, on every continent, a new face appeared.

A man who did not exist. A leader with no past. A Messiah crafted from centuries of prophecy, designed to unify the world in its darkest hour.

His voice was perfect. His words were soothing. His presence was magnetic.

He did not demand obedience. He offered peace.

And the world, desperate, afraid, fell to their knees.

Sam Watches the Lie Take Shape

From a hidden safehouse in the hills outside Jerusalem, Sam and his team watched in horror as the broadcast spread.

Denise gripped the edge of the table. "What the hell is this?"

Naomi, pale but determined, scanned the digital signatures. "It's an AI composite. A deepfake—but beyond anything we've ever seen before. The voice patterns, the facial movements, it's flawless."

Miguel's eyes darkened. "They created a false Messiah."

Marcus, still reeling from everything, looked between them. "But… people won't believe this, right?"

No one answered.

Because people were already believing it.

Crowds in Rome, in Washington, in Cairo, in Beijing—people were crying, falling to their knees, reaching for screens as if this artificial savior was truly divine.

Sam's fists clenched. They had just rewritten the ending.

"They knew this moment was coming," Naomi whispered, shaking her head. "And they had their counter-move planned years ago."

Sam took a slow breath, his mind racing. They had fought so hard to bring the truth to the surface. To wake people up.

But this?

This was a new level of deception.

Miguel turned to him. "What do we do?"

Sam exhaled, his voice steady.

"We expose it."

Naomi hesitated. "Sam… this isn't just another lie. This is a lie people want to believe."

Sam met her gaze. "Then we show them the truth they can't ignore."

Chapter Ten: The World At War

Part One: The Divide of Nations

The world had entered its final stage.

With the rise of the False Messiah, nations were forced to choose: submit to the new order or face annihilation. Protests that had once been isolated within city streets had now erupted into full-fledged revolutions. The Awakening had ignited the long-dormant fractures within global politics, exposing the deceptions that had controlled the world for centuries.

In America, the economic and social disparities that had plagued Black communities for generations now reached a boiling point. Years of marginalization, systemic denial, and being gaslit into believing that history was not theirs had created an underground resistance that no longer sought dialogue—it sought action. Cities burned, not from riots of senseless destruction, but from orchestrated defiance. The illusion of inclusion was shattered. The false promise of upward mobility, of meritocracy, of integration had been exposed as nothing more than a delaying tactic to prevent real power shifts. The so-called "American Dream" was a lie, and for the first time, people stopped pretending otherwise.

From Harlem to Atlanta, from Chicago to Detroit, Black communities—long denied access to generational wealth—began forming economic alliances of their own. New trade networks emerged, cutting out corporations that had drained their labor while giving nothing in return. Banks that had redlined them for decades collapsed overnight. The stock market reeled as an entire sector of the population refused to participate in its rigged system.

But with defiance came retaliation.

U.S. federal forces, under the guise of maintaining stability, deployed counter-insurgency units to suppress the rising economic and political shift. Protest leaders were labeled terrorists. Any attempt at self-sufficiency was deemed sedition. Social media platforms, once used to spread the Awakening's message, were seized under the guise of national security. The prophecy of Isaiah 10:1-2 echoed in the streets:

"Woe to those who decree unrighteous decrees, and to the writers who write oppression, to turn aside the needy from judgment, and to take away the right from the poor of my people."

And it wasn't just America.

In Africa, the long-exploited nations that had been looted for resources without recompense were now demanding their due. Nigeria, South Africa, Ghana, and Kenya formed a coalition, seizing foreign-owned oil fields, lithium mines, and agricultural production plants. European economies, heavily dependent on African exports, buckled under the pressure. Western nations sent diplomats under the pretense of "rebuilding trust," but everyone knew what they were truly seeking—control.

China, once a silent observer in the Awakening, now moved openly. It had long played both sides, investing in African infrastructure while maintaining ties with global banking elites. But with the Vatican-backed False Messiah rising, Beijing saw an opportunity. The old colonial powers had overplayed their hand, and China was ready to fill the vacuum they had left behind. It was no longer about alliances—it was about dominance.

But the greatest shift came in the Middle East.

The destruction of the Dome of the Rock had set fire to the entire region. What had once been seen as a localized conflict was now a war of faith, of prophecy, of identity. The leaders who had stood as gatekeepers of the old world order were now scrambling to keep control, but it was too late.

And at the center of it all, standing against the rising tide of deception, were Sam Matthews and his team.

Part Two: The Fall of Babylon

Sam watched the screen in silence. Across every major network, the False Messiah's image was omnipresent. He had been given a name—one pulled from the ancient texts, carefully chosen for psychological impact.

"Adoniel."

The name echoed across the world, spoken by presidents, kings, and religious leaders alike. But Sam knew the truth. This was not the return of a promised savior. This was the crowning of the final deception.

Denise was pacing, her arms crossed tightly over her chest. "They're moving too fast," she muttered. "It's like they already had this in place before any of this started."

Miguel scoffed. "Of course they did. You think the Vatican didn't have a contingency plan? They knew prophecy would unfold. The Obscured always had a counter-move ready."

Naomi, still recovering from her wounds, tapped furiously at her keyboard. "It's worse than just a digital takeover. The global banking system is shifting. They're phasing out all independent currencies, rolling everything into a single blockchain network. The second this goes live, every transaction, every purchase, every asset—it's all under their control."

Sam exhaled sharply. **Revelation 13:17** flashed in his mind:

"And that no one might buy or sell except he that had the mark."

Marcus, who had been silent up until now, looked up. "So this is it," he said softly. "Babylon's final trick."

Sam nodded. "And we're the only ones who can stop it."

Naomi looked up from her screen. "There's one weak point. The global economic shift is being facilitated through a Vatican-controlled AI system. If we can breach it, we can dismantle the framework before it solidifies."

Miguel frowned. "That's not going to be easy."

Denise glanced at Sam. "But it's possible."

Sam met her gaze, then looked back at the screen. Images of Adoniel, of world leaders swearing allegiance. It was all happening exactly as foretold.

He thought of the words from **Isaiah 47:1-3**:

"Come down, and sit in the dust, O virgin daughter of Babylon; sit on the ground, there is no throne… for thou shalt no more be called tender and delicate."

The kingdom they had built in deception was coming down.

And they would be the ones to bring it crashing to the ground.

Part Three: The Last Move

Sam turned to the team. "This is our only shot. If we don't act now, they'll consolidate everything.

We lose the chance to strike at the heart of their system."

Naomi pulled up a map on the screen. "The AI core is buried beneath the Vatican's archives. It's heavily guarded, but it has a vulnerability—an access point through a backup server in Rome's financial district."

Miguel cracked his knuckles. "So we hit them in their own backyard."

Denise turned to Sam. "What if this is a trap? What if they're expecting us?"

Sam exhaled. "They probably are. But that doesn't change what we have to do."

He looked at each of them, seeing the determination in their eyes. They had come too far to stop now. The world was watching, waiting for the final outcome.

Revelation 18:4 rang in his mind:

"Come out of her, my people, that ye be not partakers of her sins, and that ye receive not of her plagues."

This wasn't just about survival anymore.

This was about ending Babylon once and for all.

Sam tightened his grip on his weapon.

"It's time to bring the empire down."

Chapter Eleven: The War for Truth

Part One: The Great Deception Unraveled

The world was no longer operating under the illusion of peace.

With the emergence of Adoniel—the False Messiah—global leaders had fallen in line, swearing fealty to the new order. The Vatican declared him the final fulfillment of prophecy. Mecca's clerics called him the one sent to unite all under divine law. Presidents, prime ministers, kings—they all surrendered to the deception, and those who didn't were swiftly silenced.

But even as the nations bowed, the people had begun to rise.

From the favelas of Brazil to the streets of Lagos, from the slums of Mumbai to the neighborhoods of Detroit, an underground resistance had taken shape. The Awakening was no longer just an ideology. It was a movement, a war of revelation against the architects of deception.

Sam and his team had seen this coming.

Inside a secure location on the outskirts of Rome, they watched as the False Messiah broadcast another address. His words were smooth, perfectly calculated. AI enhancements made his face seem ethereal, his voice carry a warmth that instilled trust in the masses. But for those who knew the truth, every word was a dagger into the heart of humanity.

"I come not to destroy but to fulfill," Adoniel declared, his hands raised as he addressed the world. **"The world has been divided for too long. The time of separation has ended. The time of unity has come."**

Naomi's fingers flew across her keyboard, decoding the digital patterns behind his voice. "They've embedded neuro-linguistic programming into his speeches. It's designed to trigger compliance in people's subconscious."

Miguel clenched his fists. "They're brainwashing the world."

Denise turned to Sam. "What do we do?"

Sam exhaled slowly. The answer had been written long before this moment.

2 Thessalonians 2:11-12 had warned:

"And for this cause, God shall send them strong delusion, that they should believe a lie: that they all might be judged who believed not the truth, but had pleasure in unrighteousness."

The world had been given over to deception. But not all had fallen.

"We expose him," Sam said finally. "We tear down the illusion."

Part Two: The Fall of the Vatican's Digital Fortress

Time was running out.

Naomi brought up the Vatican's server architecture, displaying the AI core that powered Adoniel's worldwide broadcasts. "The entire neural network that sustains this deception is routed through one central hub beneath the Vatican archives. If we take it down, we sever their control."

Miguel smirked. "Then let's burn it down."

Denise shot him a look. "It won't be that easy."

And she was right.

The Vatican was the most heavily fortified location in the world. Its underground chambers, many of which were unknown to the public, housed classified archives, forbidden texts, and centuries of hidden knowledge. And now, it had become the heart of the False Messiah's empire.

Naomi continued. "There's an access tunnel beneath the Sistine Chapel, built centuries ago as an escape route for the papacy. If we can breach it, we can get inside."

Sam studied the layout. "And once we're in?"

Naomi's expression darkened. "Then we fight."

Part Three: The Battle Beneath Rome

They moved under cover of night.

The city of Rome was a ghost town, patrolled by heavily armed units loyal to the new order. Drones hovered above the skyline, scanning for dissenters. Every major broadcast played Adoniel's image on repeat, reinforcing his manufactured divinity.

Miguel led the way through the tunnels, his weapon at the ready. Sam followed closely behind, his senses sharp. Naomi and Denise moved in unison, Marcus staying close to his mother. Every step brought them closer to the heart of the deception.

As they neared the underground vault, Naomi whispered, "We're inside their perimeter."

Sam nodded. "Let's move."

But just as they turned the corner, floodlights flared to life.

A voice echoed through the chamber.

"Did you really think we wouldn't be expecting you?"

Ross.

The architect of deception himself stepped forward, flanked by a team of black-clad operatives. His smirk was laced with satisfaction. "You've been a thorn in our side for too long, Matthews."

Miguel raised his gun. "Wish I could say the same about you, but honestly, I don't think about you that much."

Ross's smirk widened. "That's cute. But it doesn't change the fact that you've already lost."

He gestured to the screens behind him, displaying live feeds of major cities around the world. Riots. Suppression. Martial law.

"You think taking down our AI will stop this? You're fools. The world doesn't want truth. They want order. And we have given it to them."

Sam took a step forward, his voice steady. "You didn't give them order. You gave them chains."

Ross's eyes gleamed. "And they welcomed them."

A beat of silence.

Then, Naomi whispered into the comms. "Now."

The entire facility shuddered.

Sirens blared. Screens flickered. The Vatican's digital fortress—Adoniel's lifeline—was crashing.

Ross's smug expression vanished. "What did you—"

Naomi's voice was ice. "We rewrote your script."

The screens behind him distorted. Adoniel's perfect face glitched. His voice warped. Then—

It collapsed.

And the world saw the lie in real time.

Part Four: The Revelation That Shakes the World

Across every major city, the image of the False Messiah disintegrated. His perfect features fractured into raw data. His voice became nothing but scrambled audio waves.

The people who had worshipped him, who had believed the lie, stared in horror.

In Mecca, clerics gasped as the face of their so-called savior vanished.

In Rome, the Pope collapsed to his knees, whispering, **"What have we done?"**

In Washington, the President watched in stunned silence as his entire administration's credibility unraveled.

And in the streets?

The people raged.

Scripture had foretold this moment. **Jeremiah 51:8**:

"Babylon is suddenly fallen and destroyed: howl for her; take balm for her pain, if so be she may be healed."

The deception had been exposed.

The empire was collapsing.

Part Five: The Final Judgment

Sam and his team stood in the wreckage of the Vatican's command center. Ross lay slumped against the console, defeated.

The battle wasn't over. But the lie had fallen. And now, the world had to choose.

Denise turned to Sam. "What happens now?"

Sam exhaled. "Now, we finish this."

Naomi pulled up one final command on her tablet. She turned to Sam. "Do it."

Sam pressed the button.

The last remnants of the False Messiah's empire crumbled. The Awakening had begun.

And the war for truth had reached its final stage.

Chapter Twelve: The Trumpet Sounds

Part One: The World Stands at the Edge

The earth trembled under the weight of its own reckoning.

The illusion had been shattered. The world had seen the lie. The False Messiah was no more. And yet, instead of salvation, chaos erupted.

From Washington to Johannesburg, from Mecca to Rio de Janeiro, entire governments fell into disarray. Some leaders tried to suppress the truth, declaring the exposure of Adoniel a cyberterrorist attack. Others fell silent, retreating into bunkers as their regimes collapsed beneath the weight of public fury.

But for the people? There was no turning back.

Across the African continent, nations erupted in both prayer and defiance. In Nigeria, crowds took to the streets shouting, **"We are the scattered! We will return!"** In Ghana, religious leaders wept as they reopened scriptures long hidden from the public. Ethiopia declared a national day of fasting, invoking **Isaiah 11:11**: *"And it shall come to pass in that day, that the Lord shall set his hand again the second time to recover the remnant of his people."*

In America, the Black churches—long the heart of resistance—became command centers. In Harlem, in Atlanta, in Detroit, in Oakland, the people gathered. Not just to protest, but to plan. Underground networks of activists and scholars worked feverishly to decode suppressed historical texts, cross-referencing ancient maps with modern genealogical data. The scattered were remembering who they were.

Sam watched from their new safehouse in the outskirts of Cairo, a secure location known only to the highest members of the Awakening.

Naomi's voice was hoarse from lack of sleep. "The world is splitting in two."

Denise rubbed her temples. "Either they believe what they saw, or they refuse to let go of the lie."

Miguel exhaled. "The ones who refuse? They won't just sit back. They'll fight to preserve their illusion."

Sam nodded, his jaw clenched. "Then so will we."

Part Two: The Nations Prepare for War

In the corridors of power, the old order was regrouping.

The Vatican was in flames—both figuratively and literally. The exposure of Adoniel had shattered its stronghold. The Pope had vanished, his closest advisors executed in the fallout. But in the depths of Rome, in a chamber beneath St. Peter's Basilica, those who had ruled in the shadows were already moving to their next phase.

Ross, bruised but alive, stood before what remained of the world's elite.

"This isn't over."

A high-ranking general from NATO stepped forward. "The world has lost faith in every government. If we don't act now, the masses will turn to something else. Something beyond our control."

A Saudi prince adjusted his robe. "The people are seeking their true identity. And when they find it, our entire system will collapse."

Ross's eyes were cold. "Then we strike before they can."

A tense silence followed. Then, a single word was spoken.

"Babylon."

And just like that, the final war was set in motion.

Part Three: The Black Exodus

Naomi's fingers shook as she read the reports coming in from every major intelligence feed.

"They're moving against the African nations first."

Sam turned sharply. "Why?"

Denise was already ahead of him, scrolling through intercepted communications. "Because that's where the resistance is strongest. The West sees Africa as the birthplace of the Awakening."

Miguel swore. "They're trying to wipe out the root."

Sam's stomach twisted. It had been prophesied.

Jeremiah 30:10: *"Fear not, O Jacob my servant, neither be dismayed, O Israel: for, lo, I will save thee from afar, and thy seed from the land of their captivity."*

Zephaniah 3:10: *"From beyond the rivers of Ethiopia my suppliants, even the daughter of my dispersed, shall bring mine offering."*

He turned to Naomi. "We need a plan."

She swallowed hard. "We don't just need a plan. We need a miracle."

Part Four: The Trumpet Sounds

In the ruins of the Vatican, Ross gave the final order.

"Launch Omega."

Across the world, black sites activated.

- In Nigeria, missiles targeted key resistance hubs. • In Brazil, leaders of the Awakening were assassinated in coordinated strikes. • In South Africa, an emergency lockdown was declared, cutting off all external communication. • In America, drones hovered above Black-majority cities, awaiting the command to suppress the coming uprising.

The war had begun.

And at that moment, the sky above Jerusalem burned.

Part Five: The Cliffhanger

The world stood still.

A live broadcast cut across every channel. Every screen, every device, every nation.

A single figure stood on the Temple Mount.

Not Adoniel.

A new man.

His robes were stained with blood, his eyes burning with something ancient. His voice—powerful, steady—echoed across the land.

Zechariah 14:4: *"And his feet shall stand in that day upon the mount of Olives, which is before Jerusalem on the east."*

"The time of judgment has come."

A deafening silence followed. And then, the earth shook.

Sam, watching from Cairo, felt the air shift. The final prophecy was upon them.

Miguel whispered, "What the hell was that?"

Naomi turned to them, her face pale.

"It's Him."

The screen glitched, then cut to black.

And across the world, every person who had refused to see, refused to hear, refused to believe—

Fell to their knees.

End of *Final Exodus: The Reckoning*

TO BE CONTINUED IN:

Final Exodus: The Uprising

Coming Soon

The war **was never just about deception.**

It was about **control.**

The unseen ruler may have retreated, but **his influence still lingers.** Governments **rebuild in secret.** Old powers **re-emerge.** And those who once knelt **are already preparing to rise again.**

But this time—**humanity is ready.**

Sam and his team are no longer just survivors.

They are **leaders.**

And as the world takes its first steps toward true freedom, **new enemies rise from the shadows.**

The next battle **is not for survival.**

It is for dominion.

The **Final Exodus** continues.

The Uprising has begun.

Appendix: The Biblical, Historical, and Scientific Case for the Descendants of Slavery as Israelites

Introduction: Why This Matters

The question of Israelite identity has been a topic of theological, historical, and genetic debate for centuries. This appendix is not intended to attack or diminish any group but rather to explore a historical perspective often overlooked. The goal is to examine whether the Black descendants of slavery—particularly those scattered through the transatlantic slave trade—align with the biblical, historical, and scientific descriptions of Israel.

This discussion does not seek to discredit Jewish identity but rather to highlight that the **biblical Israelites were a dispersed people, and their descendants exist in various parts of the world.** This is in line with the prophecy of Israel's scattering and regathering.

1 ⬜ Biblical Evidence: The Lost and Scattered Tribes

A. The Curses of Deuteronomy 28

One of the strongest biblical arguments for the Black descendants of slavery as Israelites comes from Deuteronomy 28, where Moses outlines blessings for obedience and curses for disobedience. Among the curses are prophecies that closely match the historical experiences of Black people during the transatlantic slave trade.

Deuteronomy 28:68 (LXX - Septuagint) "And the Lord shall bring thee back into Egypt in ships, by the way whereof I said unto thee, 'Thou shalt see it no more again'; and there ye shall be sold unto your enemies for bondmen and bondwomen, and no man shall buy you."

- **Egypt in this context symbolizes bondage (Exodus 20:2).** The prophecy describes Israelites being taken to slavery by ships—a direct parallel to the transatlantic slave trade.
- **"Sold unto your enemies"** describes a people taken into captivity and treated as property.
- **"No man shall buy you"** (redeem you) refers to the inability to escape oppression despite numerous struggles for freedom.

B. Scattering and Forgetting Their Identity

Jeremiah 17:4 (LXX - Septuagint) "And thou shalt even thyself discontinue from thine heritage that I gave thee; and I will cause thee to serve thine enemies in a land which thou knowest not."

- This prophecy states that Israel would **lose their heritage** and serve their oppressors in foreign lands. The forced cultural erasure of enslaved Africans aligns with this prophecy.

Luke 21:24 "And they shall fall by the edge of the sword, and shall be led away captive into all nations."

- Christ prophesied that Israelites would be **led away captive into all nations** after Jerusalem's destruction in 70 A.D. Many scholars, including Flavius Josephus, record that Israelites fled into Africa.

---

2 ▢ Historical Evidence: Israel's Migration into Africa

A. The 70 A.D. Diaspora and African Migration

After the **destruction of the Second Temple** in 70 A.D. by the Romans, many Israelites fled **southward into Africa.**

- **Flavius Josephus**, a 1st-century Jewish historian, wrote that the Romans enslaved and scattered Israelites into various parts of the world.
- Many scholars note that Israelites took refuge in Africa, blending with indigenous populations over centuries.
- By the time of the transatlantic slave trade (1400s–1800s), many of these Israelites were among those captured and sold into slavery.

B. The Slave Trade Targeted Israelites

The transatlantic slave trade systematically captured people from regions where **Israelite presence had been recorded.**

- **Portuguese Slave Records**: Early European accounts describe captives from **West Africa (Benin, Ghana, Nigeria, etc.)** as "Jews of the Guinea."
- **The Kingdom of Judah**: A 1747 map of West Africa by Emmanuel Bowen labels a region as "The Kingdom of Juda" in modern-day Benin, reinforcing historical connections.
- **Islamic Slave Trade Accounts**: Arab traders in the 8th–14th centuries described capturing "black Jews" in Africa.

3 ☐ Scientific Evidence: Genetic and Cultural Links

A. The Lemba People and the Kohanim Gene

The **Lemba people** of southern Africa claim Israelite descent. Genetic studies confirm their oral history.

- **DNA studies (Tudor Parfitt, 1999)** found that the Lemba carry the **Cohen Modal Haplotype (CMH),** a genetic marker

associated with the priestly line of Aaron (Kohanim).
- **Their customs—kosher slaughter, circumcision on the 8th day, and oral traditions—mirror biblical Israelite practices.**

B. The Igbo and Other African Tribes

- The **Igbo of Nigeria** maintain **Torah-based practices** and claim descent from Gad, Asher, and other tribes.
- Genetic testing on African Americans has shown significant markers connecting them to these tribes.

4 ☐ How This Ties to the Second Exodus and Biblical Prophecy

A. The Awakening of the Lost Tribes

Isaiah 11:11-12 "And it shall come to pass in that day, that the Lord shall set his hand again the second time to recover the remnant of his people... and shall assemble the outcasts of Israel, and gather together the dispersed of Judah from the four corners of the earth."

- This prophecy describes a **Second Exodus**, where the scattered Israelites will awaken and return.

- The modern "awakening" movement—where Black descendants of slavery are reclaiming their Israelite identity—fits this prophecy.

B. Tying It to Real-World Geopolitics

- The **Black struggle for economic, social, and political justice** aligns with biblical prophecies about Israel's suffering and restoration.
- **DEI rollbacks, police brutality, and economic disparities** reflect the oppression prophesied in scripture.
- The **push for reparations parallels Exodus 3:21**, where the Israelites left Egypt with compensation.

Final Thoughts: What This Means

This research suggests that **the descendants of the transatlantic slave trade are likely part of the biblical Israelite diaspora.** However, recognizing this truth does not mean exclusion or division. As Isaiah 56:6-8 states: "My house shall be called a house of prayer for all people."

The **awakening of the true Israelites** does not diminish others but brings restoration to a people who have been denied their heritage.

Further Reading and References:

- **Flavius Josephus, "The Wars of the Jews"**
- **Tudor Parfitt, "The Lost Tribes of Israel"**
- **Arthur Koestler, "The Thirteenth Tribe"**
- **DNA studies on the Lemba and Igbo peoples**
- **Historical slave trade records (Portuguese and British archives)**

This research is provided **for scholarly reflection and historical inquiry,** not for exclusion or division. The truth shall set us free (John 8:32).

Made in the USA
Columbia, SC
18 April 2025